W9-BYJ-776

EAST NORTHPORT PUBLIC LIBRARY
EAST NORTHPORT, NEW YORK

PIRATE
TREASURE
HUNT!

PIRATE TREASURE HUNT!

By Jan Peck

Illustrated by Adrian Tans

PELICAN PUBLISHING COMPANY

Gretna 2008

For
Captain Hooked on Ye Books, David R. Davis
—JP

For my dad,
who has sailed the high seas
and the narrow marsh creeks.
—AT

Copyright © 2008
By Jan Peck

Illustrations copyright © 2008
By Adrian Tans
All rights reserved

The word "Pelican" and the depiction of a pelican are trademarks
of Pelican Publishing Company, Inc., and are registered in the
U.S. Patent and Trademark Office.

Library of Congress Cataloging-in-Publication Data

Peck, Jan.
 Pirate treasure hunt! / by Jan Peck ; illustrated by Adrian Tans.
   p. cm.
 Summary: Captain Dare and his newly hired mates set out in search of treasure,
swimming through a lagoon, swinging through a jungle, and other obstacles before
finding the treasure, until a mouse frightens the Captain into retreat.
 ISBN 978-1-58980-549-1 (hardcover : alk. paper) [1. Imagination—Fiction. 2. Pi-
rates—Fiction. 3. Treasure hunt (Game)—Fiction.] I. Tans, Adrian, ill. II. Title.
 PZ7.P33455Pi 2008
 [E]—dc22

                    2008006326

Printed in Korea
Published by Pelican Publishing Company, Inc.
1000 Burmaster Street, Gretna, Louisiana 70053

PIRATE TREASURE HUNT!

⛵

WANTED: PIRATES
No experience or bath needed.

Ahoy, me hearties. I be Captain Dare.
So, ye wanna go on a pirate treasure hunt, do ye?
Ye think ye have the guts?
If ye wanna go, say "Aye, aye, Captain."
Aye, aye, Captain.

Arrrrrrrrh! That sounded like some lily-
    livered landlubber.
Say it like a *real pirate*.
Aye, aye, Captain!
That's better. Now repeat after me . . .
    And none of that whining or hollering.
Cause we be goin' on a *pirate treasure hunt!*

Going on a treasure hunt.
  Going on a treasure hunt.
Searching for the pirate's cave.
  Searching for the pirate's cave.
We're so smart. **We're so smart.**
And we're so brave. **And we're so brave.**

Coming to a lagoon. **Coming to a lagoon.**
Can't go over it. **Can't go over it.**
Can't go under it. **Can't go under it.**
Can't go around it. **Can't go around it.**

C'mon, ye little bubble bath takers. We'll have
  to wade through it.
We'll have to wade through it.
Squishy squashy. **Squishy squashy.**

Watch out for the snapping crocodile!
Arrrrrrrrh! Big lagoon! **Big lagoon!**

Going on a treasure hunt.
Going on a treasure hunt.
Searching for the pirate's hold.
Searching for the pirate's hold.
We're so brave. **We're so brave.**
And we're so bold. **And we're so bold.**

Coming to a jungle. **Coming to a jungle.**
Can't go over it. **Can't go over it.**
Can't go under it. **Can't go under it.**
Can't go around it. **Can't go around it.**

C'mon, ye little milk sippers. We'll have to
   swing through it.
We'll have to swing through it.
Whee! Whoo! **Whee! Whoo!**

Watch out for the growling jaguar!
Arrrrrrrrh! Big jungle! **Big jungle!**

Going on a treasure hunt.
  Going on a treasure hunt.
Searching for the pirate's loot.
  Searching for the pirate's loot.
We're so bold. **We're so bold.**
And we're so cute. **And we're so cute.**

Coming to a snake pit. **Coming to a snake pit.**
Can't go over it. **Can't go over it.**
Can't go under it. **Can't go under it.**
Can't go around it. **Can't go around it.**

C'mon, ye little tooth brushers. We'll have to
  sneak across it.
We'll have to sneak across it.
Shhhh, tippy toe. **Shhhh, tippy toe.**

Watch out for the slithering snakes!
Arrrrrrrrh! Big snake pit! **Big snake pit!**

Going on a treasure hunt.
Going on a treasure hunt.
Searching for the pirate's prize.
Searching for the pirate's prize.
We're so cute. **We're so cute.**
And we're so wise. **And we're so wise.**

Coming to a cliff. **Coming to a cliff.**
Can't go over it. **Can't go over it.**
Can't go under it. **Can't go under it.**
Can't go around it. **Can't go around it.**

C'mon, ye clean sock wearers. We'll have
to climb up it.
We'll have to climb up it.
Scritchy scratchy. **Scritchy scratchy.**

Watch out for the flapping buzzard!
Arrrrrrrrh! Big cliff! **Big cliff!**

Coming to the treasure.
   Coming to the treasure.
X marks the spot. **X marks the spot.**
Can't go over it. **Can't go over it.**
Can't go under it. **Can't go under it.**
Can't go around it. **Can't go around it.**

Grab ye shovels, ye little pajama wearers.
   We'll have to dig it.
We'll have to dig it.
Dig, dig! **Dig, dig!**

Arrrrrrrrh! Big treasure chest!
   Big treasure chest!

Captain Dare, what do you see though your spyglass?
Eeeeeeeeekkkk! A mouse!

Grab ye treasure chest.
Grab ye treasure chest.

Down the cliff. **Down the cliff.**
Scritchy scratchy. **Scritchy scratchy.**

Across the snake pit.
Across the snake pit.
Shhhh, tippy toe.
Shhhh, tippy toe.

Through the jungle.
Through the jungle.
Whee! Whoo!
Whee! Whoo!

Wade the lagoon. **Wade the lagoon.**
Squishy squashy. **Squishy squashy.**

Arrrrrrrrh! Avast! We're back on our
gallant ship!
**Oh, Captain Dare, were you
scared of that little mouse?**
Shiver me timbers! Who, me?

Hoist the Jolly Roger Flag, ye little
ear scrubbers.
Set the sails. Step lively, me maties.
**Captain, what do we have in
our treasure chest?**

Arrrrrrrrh! A whole treasure load
of books!
And what is the key to opening
ye treasure?

Reading, me hearties!
Avast! Say it like a *real pirate*.
Aaaarrrrreading!